Short Stories About Giving Care

by

Elise Mathis and Mimi Mathis R.N.

Illustrated by Lilly Mathis

Short Stories About Giving Care

This book is a work of fiction. While the names, characters, places, and incidents are a product of the authors' imagination, the medical conditions are accurate and have been used to further the stories.

Book cover art by Darene Bingham Loyd

Published by Mimi Mathis

www.aboutgivingcare.com

This book is dedicated to all the Health Care Aides around the world.

Table of Contents

Dementia

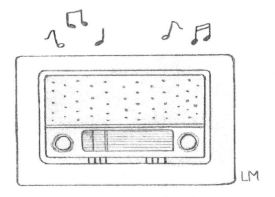

My wife has dementia. We fought it for three years, and that was part of our problem. We were so busy fighting this devastating disease that I forgot about the quality of life.

I hope our story will help others.

My name is James Green. My wife's name is Janis. I don't mean to sound cliché, but I fell in love with her the first time we met. She was a gorgeous blonde with dancing blue eyes, and she had a great capacity to love that made her irresistible.

We didn't have any children, so it was always the two of us. I taught high school science, and Janis taught first grade. She was Teacher of the Year and had also won other teaching awards.

We retired May 2015 and were making plans to travel and see the world. But when dementia hit her, it hit hard, savaging her brain before we had a chance to travel. I'd heard that its victims keep their personalities. However, that was eventually stolen from Janis too.

"Turn that thing off," she yelled at me in a voice that wasn't hers.

"What's wrong with you? Are you sick? The Cardinals are playing the Mets!"

She reached out her hands like she wanted to grab me, then dropped them. They hung at her side, open and hopeless, like the expression on her face.

Within weeks, she had increased memory loss, forgetfulness, and difficulty finding the right word. She lost interest in the things she enjoyed: cooking, singing, dancing, and talking on the phone with her friends. She didn't want to go anywhere and stayed in bed during the day. I thought she was depressed, and she was. That is part of the disease.

I made a doctor's appointment for her. She was seen the next day and went through all the tests related to mental functioning, blood tests, brain scans, and a psychiatric evaluation.

When her doctor told us the diagnosis was dementia, she was the one who took it bravely; she was remarkable—I wasn't.

I was shocked, sad, embarrassed, angry, and other negative emotions. I felt a sense of urgency to get another professional opinion. I did. Her diagnosis remained the same. I was determined to find Janis the best possible treatment. I did. There were no signs of improvement.

Within six months she lost her ability to focus, her sweet disposition, her interest in food; and she rarely talked. Too many losses too fast.

I cried a lot when she wasn't looking at me and had trouble sleeping at night. What was I going to do? What would she do if I was the one with dementia? Stupid question—I knew the answer. *To have and to hold from this day forward, for better, for worse, for richer, for poorer, in sickness and in health, to love and to cherish until we are parted by death. This is my solemn vow.*

I stayed with Janis 24 hours a day. Before she became ill, she was fond of saying that nothing stays the same. As usual, she was right. I found myself in a role reversal. She was the one who loved to cook and take care of our home. Now it was my turn.

Stress had overtaken me. I became exhausted. This disease was now robbing me of my health too. It had also taken most of our savings. I decided to use what was left to pay for some care for Janis at home. I wanted to find someone trained, insured, and bonded, so I called a local Licensed Private Care Agency. That afternoon, a nurse came and evaluated Janis. I felt some of the stress leaving me by the time she had left our home.

The next day, in walked Ellen Bright, Home Care Aide.

When Ellen met Janis, Ellen smiled at her with a beaming smile like one of Janis' first-grade students.

Janis smiled back.

"Let's all go sit and talk," Ellen said, gently taking Janis by the hand. They walked slowly together to the living room.

I followed as soon as the tears cleared from my eyes.

Ellen asked us to sit where she could face us both when she talked. We all sat down.

Ellen smiled that first-grade smile again. "Let me know if either of you have questions about my duties listed on the Care Plan. I want to make everything normal and peaceful for you both. And I'd like us to have a little fun on the way there."

I glanced at Janis and was shocked. She was nodding her head yes.

"I have an idea," Ellen said with eyes to match her last name.

"What is it?" I immediately asked.

She pointed to our radio, covered in dust, sitting on a shelf in the corner of the room.

"Music is a magic mechanism." She paused and looked directly at Janis. "What kind of music do you like,

Janis?"

"Big…big…band," she replied. "Let's hear…now."

It took me a few seconds to get over the shock of Janis talking to Ellen. I turned on the radio and found our favorite station. We were soon listening to the Tommy Dorsey Band playing *I'm Getting Sentimental Over You.*

Suddenly, a surge of nostalgia touched my heart. I stood, took Janis by the hand, and asked her to dance.

She nodded yes as her beautiful blue eyes sparkled.

The music twirled and swirled around us like magic. She rested her head on my chest as we gently swayed back and forth to the dreamy, melodic voice of Jo Stafford singing:

"Never thought I'd fall,

But now I hear love call,

I'm getting sentimental over you

Things you say and do,

Just thrill me through and through,

I'm getting sentimental over you."

Then, came the day. "I'm not sure how much longer I can keep Janis home," I said to Ellen, my voice cracking with emotions. "It may be tomorrow or three days or three weeks. But no matter when it happens, I want you to know that you showed us how to live one day at a time and gave us back the quality of life that we once cherished."

Heart Disease

> Male Home Care Aide. Flexible hours working with an elderly man. 40-hour training available.

I applied for the job and got hired before I walked out of the agency's front door that day.

My name is Tim Finley, and I'm going to school to become a Nurse Practitioner. I qualified for the job without having to complete their training course. The number of hours and the time being on duty were just what I needed for my school schedule.

My assignment was Mr. Thompson, a 93-year-old man who lived alone. The R.N. who reviewed the Care Plan with me said that Mr. Thompson fired the last three women they sent him. She said maybe sending a male should be the answer to this difficult situation.

Mr. Thompson needed help with bathing, housekeeping, shopping for groceries, laundry, and preparing supper meals. He had a history of a heart attack, a heart valve replacement, and most recently, chronic congestive heart failure and kidney failure.

My dad had a heart attack, two stents, then open heart by-pass surgery, so I had firsthand experience in caring for a heart patient. My dad died when I was fifteen. He always called me "Pal." We loved going fishing and playing baseball. I think about him daily and still miss him.

I looked forward to my new job. Mr. Thompson was my first home care assignment, and I felt confident about my ability to do a good job. Giving one-on-one care, instead of taking care of acutely ill patients in a hospital, should be a piece of cake. But that was what I thought before I met Mr. Thompson.

Mr. Thompson lived in a small duplex on the edge of town. His neighbor checked up on him daily.

The first day on duty, the entry door stood wide open. I rang the doorbell.

"I'm on my way there," a trembling voice called out.

A few minutes later, Mr. Thompson met me at the screen door. He was using a walker and wore a pair of overalls with gaping holes in the legs. He had dark, piercing brown eyes and a scraggly, long gray beard.

"Come on in," he said.

I walked inside and extended my arm for a handshake. He reeked of body odor. "I'm Tim Finley. Please call me Tim," I said politely.

He clenched his hands on his walker, ignoring my

15

invitation to shake hands. "Call me by my name— Mr. Thompson," he said with a firm but quivering tone.

I glanced around his home. It was a mess, and it smelled horrid. Newspapers were strewn all over the living room floor, and the kitchen looked disgusting. I saw garbage bags piled in the corner, and there was enough dried food on the floor for a meal. I caught myself staring at the filth and quickly looked back at him.

"I have a copy of your Care Plan. Would you like to go over it with me?" I asked.

"No, I'd like you to start cleaning the bathroom, then clean the kitchen. It has been days since your agency that provides consistent and loving care has sent me any help."

"You realize I'm only going to be here for two hours from 9 am to 11 am Monday through Friday?"

He lifted his forefinger and pointed down a short hall. "The bathroom is that way. If you want to work with the elderly, don't be so mouthy."

The bathroom made me gag. It smelled like urine. Streaks of dried feces were on the floor. It took me 45 minutes of scrubbing, chipping, and cleaning before it was sanitary.

My next challenge was the kitchen. Besides the dirty floor, there were dirty dishes on the cabinet and thick lumps of grease around the stove. Meals on Wheels boxes with left-over moldy food sat on the table, and the sink was full of filthy pots and pans.

When I was scrubbing and washing the pots and pans, Mr. Thompson hollered out, "Young man...you can hang around here, but that racket has got to go!"

I continued to work as quietly as possible. When I left that day, I was tired and ready to get out of there.

The second week on duty, Mr. Thompson told me he wanted to shower. I scrubbed him clean, and he even asked me to wash the fringe of gray hair around his bald scalp. I soon learned he was the decision-maker, and when I asked him about his family, or what he did to make a living, he repeatedly said he'd tell me later.

As time passed, I became concerned about the increased swelling in his feet and ankles. He was coughing a lot, and when he walked, only a short distance, he became extremely short of breath. I was sure fluid was building up in his lungs. I notified the R.N. Supervisor and urged him to see his doctor or have his neighbor take him to Urgent Care. I assured him that I would go with them, but he refused in his unique manner.

"Use your head for something besides wearing a hat. I'm old, have a bad heart, and kidney failure. The only thing a doctor can do to help me is to give me a big triple-dose of morphine, and I'm not ready for that."

Maybe he was right, but I wanted him to get better. I had grown to like him a lot.

The next day, when I was changing his sheets, I saw a picture on his bedside of two men fishing. One was Mr. Thompson, and the other one looked like him but younger. I didn't say anything to him about the picture, but I decided to ask him to go fishing with me. He had a wheelchair that we could use, and I wanted to take him to the fishing spot where my dad used to take me. I talked to the R.N. Supervisor about my idea and got permission.

To my surprise, he said yes.

It was sunny, 74 degrees with a nice breeze blowing. I pushed Mr. Thompson in the wheelchair to my favorite fishing spot on the river. The sky was a clear blue

18

as the rippling river sparkled and flickered jigsaw patterns on top of the water.

"It's a good day for fishing," I said.

He coughed and cleared his throat. "Every day is a good day for fishing."

Within fifteen minutes, we caught five small bass and one large crappie. We threw them back in. After that, I sat on the ground in front of the wheelchair and talked. I thanked him for fishing with me, talked about my father, and told him my father was my *pal*. I also told him about my plans to be a Nurse Practitioner. He didn't respond. At one point, we sat quietly listening to birds chirping as we breathed in the fresh air, just enjoying nature.

After a few minutes, he broke the silence. "It's nice here, but I'm tired and hungry, and we can't eat the scenery."

He didn't say a word on the way back to his home.

At 7:00 am Monday, my supervisor sent me a text message: *Call me asap.*

I immediately called her.

"Tim, I'm sorry to tell you that Mr. Thompson died

Saturday. They found a piece of paper next to him. It was a note written to you. Come by the office when you have time and get it." There was a long pause. "Tim, I want you to know that you did an excellent job for him."

I gasped and tried to speak, but no words came out. Tears flooded my eyes. I swallowed hard. "I'll be there at 8:00."

The supervisor was waiting for me in the front office. She handed me an envelope, hugged me, then said, "Mr. Thompson's neighbor told us that Mr. Thompson was a retired mechanic. We knew his wife died ten years ago, but we didn't know they had one child, a son. His son died three years ago, and his name was Tim."

When I got in my car, I opened the envelope. As I read his note, it was as if I could hear his voice speaking the words.

Tim,

You're a fine young man. Thanks for taking me fishing. Your father would be proud of you. You'll be an excellent Nurse Practitioner.

Your pal,

Short Stories About Giving Care

J.T. Thompson

Housekeeping with Ms. Alacenia

Ms. Alacenia was the sweetest lady I had ever known. From the moment I met her, I knew she had a story to tell; her eyes said it all. She was kind, generous, and had the smoothest Southern accent in all of Alabama. She was the reason I woke up excited to go to work. She taught me half of what I know, and I owe my organization and cleaning skills to her. It all started when I almost lost my job. The client I was helping said I was good at everything but housekeeping, and she wanted another aide.

After that happened, the R.N. Supervisor reviewed some housekeeping skills with me and assigned me to Ms. Alacenia.

It was my first day with Ms. Alacenia, and I was nervous because of my recent experience. She knew what time I would be there and had the door unlocked. I walked in, and the smell of fresh biscuits filled the house. She was sitting at the table with a warm, welcoming presence. My fear slowly started to fade away as I approached the table and took a seat. She could tell something was wrong, and I suspected she knew what happened to me in my last job.

"What's keepin' you down sugar?" Ms. Alacenia asked with the sweetest twang in her voice.

"Oh, I don't want to worry you. It's nothing."

"Darlin' I know when something is wrong, and trust me, you are not yourself today."

"Well, the thing is...I'm nervous about housekeeping. I don't want to fail at this job and have to leave you. I know I've only been here a short time, but

23

honestly, I can already tell I want to work for you," I blurted out without stopping to take a breath.

"Oh, sugar, you came to the right place."

"What?"

"Baby, I used to clean for a-livin', and I don't mind one bit in helpin' you."

I just looked at her and smiled.

She stood up and positioned herself on her walker, and we got down to business.

"Now listen, the first step is to organize your supplies. You don't want your stuff looking like a tornado ran right through. If you keep your stuff cluttered, then you are going to waste half your time searching for supplies."

We got to work putting my plastic bucket in the bathroom and stocked it with cleaner for the tub, toilet cleaning supplies, glass cleaner, rags, and gloves.

"Okay, what's next?" I asked, excited to clean.

"Next, you need to clear all the clutter out before you start cleaning. For example, you can throw away these old newspapers. Just ask me what I want to keep or throw away."

"Hey, I'm getting the hang of this Ms. Alacenia."

"I knew you would, sugar. Now the third step is always to work efficiently. Spray what you need to dust when you go into the room. That gives your cleaning products time to work the best. Also, don't pick up any treasures or special novelty items to clean under them, because you don't want to break anything. Besides that, the nurse that came here told me it's their rule to clean around them. She also said that you could only do light housekeeping; you're not a heavy cleaning service."

"Is that all?"

"Almost. Just remember to clean from top to bottom. You are likely going to get dust on the floor, so you don't want to have to vacuum twice." She finished with a grin.

After I had cleaned the assigned areas, we sat down on the couch and looked at each other with a sense of accomplishment.

"Thank you so much. I don't know what I would have done without you," I said.

"You're welcome. I like you and want you to come back sugar."

The Fall

She recently sold her farmland and the lovely old home that had she lived in for 63 years. She knew she had no choice. Her bones were severely brittle, and she was tired. Monday morning the movers were coming, and she was going to live in an assisted living facility, Sunrise Meadows.

It was Friday night, and she planned to enjoy an evening of total independence, peace, and solitude. Everything was packed, except a few treasured items.

27

Her husband died 15 years ago. She had only one daughter who she called a Vulture. The name was appropriate because her daughter liked to gain from other people's troubles, including her mother's. The only time she visited her mother was to take something from her: money, food, or items in the home that she swore her beloved father gave her before he died.

The woman didn't tell her daughter that she had opened a trust at the bank, and all the money from selling her farm and home would go to pay for her assisted living, and to the local animal shelter.

The woman was sad about moving, but most of her close neighbors had died, except her 81-year-old friend, Maryanne. Four months ago, Maryanne turned into a Cougar and married a 66-year-old man. The man promised to love Maryanne and take care of her if she would "will him" everything she owns. Maryanne agreed. The man had a stroke two months later, became disabled, and now Maryanne is taking care of him.

The woman began thinking about her own future. Suddenly, her daughter's "smart mouth" remarks popped into her mind. Her daughter told her that the 100th Monkey

Theory was true about old people who lived in places like Sunrise Assisted Living. She said that in a few days her mother would be like that 100th monkey and mimic the other 99 old people living there. The woman hadn't meant to think that. She shook her head and envisioned all the nice amenities waiting for her at her new home.

She retreated to her bedroom and shut the door. She was ready to pack the rest of her treasured items that she hid from her daughter. She walked across the carpet with deliberate steps and opened the closet door. Ever so slowly, she looked up and reached for the large box on the shelf. Without warning, she felt dizzy, and the room started spinning. She lost her balance and fell flat on her back!

In a state of shock, she held her breath, then burst out crying. Her right arm and leg hurt. She tried to move her arm, but it was too painful. She cried out again as another severe pain rushed into her head. It radiated through her right hip and groin. She clamped her teeth to make herself stop crying, lifted her head slowly, and glanced at her right leg. Her right foot was positioned on its side, and her right leg looked shorter than the left one. The pain speared her again. Her heartbeat hammered in her chest. She gasped for air and tried to sit up, but the pain in

29

her arm engulfed her. She wept again, and a deep sadness consumed her.

Unable to bring a thought to completion, she placed her left hand on her heart. Her Lifeline pendant was in perfect position around her neck. She pressed the button, took a long, deep breath, closed her eyes, and prayed.

Handwashing

Dr. Ignaz Semmelweis

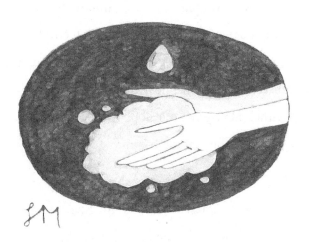

T he sweat continued to drip down my forehead and into my eyes. My hair was a tangled mess, and my face felt as if it was a hot summer's day, even though it was the middle of January.

The year was 1847, and I was in the Maternity Department of the Vienna General Hospital. I had been having labor pains all day, and at times it felt like a thousand daggers stabbing into my abdomen. Seconds felt like an eternity. I tried to relax between pains, but all I could hear was crying and screaming from the other mothers in the ward. This was my first child, and I felt every emotion an expecting mother could have. The only time I relaxed was when I heard a newborn baby crying for the first time. That gave me hope until I looked at the girl standing in the corner of the room.

She was young, and she couldn't have been working at the hospital for too long. She was probably a student, and clearly, she hadn't learned how to hide her emotions. She looked at me with this look on her face like it was the last time anyone was going to see me. Then I scanned the room and saw another young hospital worker glaring at me in the same way. *Stop looking at me like that,* I thought.

Then, I heard someone say another mother was

dead.

I looked to the nurse helping me with my head swimming in fear. My heart started racing. I could feel my palms sweating, and my labor pains were getting stronger.

"You're going to have to try to relax. We need you to work with us."

"I'm…I'm sorry, but I heard someone say that another mother was dead!" I couldn't control myself. I was too nervous. However, the nurse didn't respond, but her eyes said it all. My situation was normal. She had seen that happen before, and she expected me to meet the same fate. Could I die before I even see my baby? Can everyone please stop looking at me with that awful look?

Then Dr. Ignaz Semmelweis walked in to deliver my baby. He had a difficult presence to read but little did I know he would save my life and many others.

That was nearly 20 years ago today, and as I look across the room at my daughter holding her newborn son, I can't help feeling forever indebted to Dr. Semmelweis, who saved my life.

There had been an increasingly large number of

mothers who had been dying after childbirth. Doctors would go from task to task, including autopsies, without washing their hands and spread all kinds of germs. Dr. Semmelweis had an idea that if the hospital staff just started washing their hands and cleaning their tools in-between procedures, it would cause a decrease in the deaths of new mothers.

I was the first woman who the new practice was implemented on, and I was able to see my baby grow up because of him. He saved me with three simple words, *wash your hands.*

Years later, I went back to the hospital to thank him in person but was told he had been mocked and ridiculed, and eventually pushed out of practice.

"What do you mean pushed out?" I questioned one particular man behind the desk more focused on his papers than he was on my question.

"A lot of the doctors made his life miserable all because he thought washing hands would help prevent deaths."

"But I am living proof that he was right."

"You and many others. Listen, he was right, but the other doctors didn't want to admit they were wrong. It was a terrible mess. Dr. Semmelweis was incredibly hostile towards the other doctors, and no one would listen to each other. Now I must get back to my job. If you want to find out more, you can go visit the asylum where he died," he said while walking away.

"Asylum..." I whispered as he strutted off, but my words seem to trail off with him.

Dr. Semmelweis saved me and many others, and now he is just a forgotten thought.

--Maria Konstantin, 1866

The Flood

Mrs. Smith was a sweet lady, and she reminded me a lot of one of my great-aunts. I had been working with her for quite some time, and most days were spent doing our routine, but once a week we would go on our special grocery store trips. Mrs. Smith loved getting out of the house and looking out the window on the car ride there. On Thursday, Mrs. Smith was particularly excited to go

36

because she was going to make a homemade pie for her grandson who was coming to visit.

I had checked the weather that morning, like I do every time we go out, to be safe. It called for rain; however, I knew it was important for Mrs. Smith to go, so we loaded up into the car. There were dark clouds overhead, but when I turned and saw the smile on her face, I pulled out of the driveway and headed to the store.

We were only in the store for a few minutes. When we came out, a brilliant flash of lightning hit the ground, then thunder rumbled in the darkened sky. We quickly got in the car. I pulled it around and started driving home.

The rain started pouring down. It was pounding on the windshield, and I could barely see. I heard my cell phone go off with a flash-flood warning. My hands were shaking, and I could feel my heart pumping fast. I was terrified. Then I remembered the big dip straight ahead in the road. *Turn around, don't drown* flashed across my mind. I decided to pull over and turn around.

After I turned the car around, I noticed something strange. The floor was wet. The water was quickly spilling in from the outside. The car stalled! I turned toward Mrs.

Smith and could see the terror in her eyes. I scanned my brain for answers. All I could think was to get to higher ground.

"Listen, Mrs. Smith, we need to get on top of the car," I yelled over the pounding of the rain.

"I don't know if you remember, but I'm 87 years old. I can't climb onto a car!"

"We are going to have to try. If we wait much longer, we could drown in the car."

We both looked down at the floor and saw the water rising. It was above our ankles now and getting higher with each passing second. She looked at me and nodded. I opened my door first. I got out and waded into the rushing water over to her side of the car. I opened her door and helped her get out. The rain kept pouring down, and the raging water grew stronger. I held on to her tightly and lifted her onto the hood of the car. It was difficult, but she knew she didn't have an option.

We slipped around the car until we made it to the top. Drenched in the rain and shivering cold, we just sat there holding each other tight. I thought this was going to be the end, but I kept reassuring her it was going to be okay. Water was running down my face, but I couldn't tell if it was the rain or my tears.

Suddenly, we could hear sirens in the distance. Through the downpour, we saw a flickering red light. It was a flashing red emergency light on a fire truck. And the fire truck was heading toward us! We just looked at each other and smiled.

Elder Abuse

My name is Kate. I've been a Home Care Aide for one year and like the work most of the time. One of the times when I didn't like my job was when I took care of Emma, an attractive 75-year-old woman who lived alone. Emma was sweet and very forgetful. She needed help with housekeeping and personal care. She was homebound and didn't have any family living nearby. A retired neighbor picked up groceries for her and did "handyman" work for her.

The first day I met the neighbor, there was something about him that I didn't like. He seemed a little creepy to me. He told me Emma didn't need my services because she wanted him to take care of her. When I mentioned what he said to Emma, she didn't respond.

Two days later, when I went to Emma's home, the neighbor wasn't there, and I was relieved. That day, I noticed a change in Emma's behavior. I barely got a smile or a glance from her, and she was walking slower than the first time I was with her. I became concerned and stayed close by her side.

A little later that day, Emma told me she was ready to take her shower. As I assisted her onto the shower chair, I saw some large bruises on the inside of her upper thighs. They weren't there the last time I helped her bathe.

When I asked Emma what happened, she got tears in her eyes and told me the neighbor did it.

I felt sick to my stomach. I didn't want to get involved. I knew it would be the neighbor's word against hers. I wanted to run away. I remembered what happened to

41

me. No one told the truth.

Neither of us said a word as I helped her get dressed. We walked in silence to the living room. She sat on the couch. I turned on the T.V. and handed her the remote control. I told her I'd be right back and quietly left the room.

I locked the front door, took my cell phone out of my pocket, and called my supervisor. I told her what I saw and what Emma told me. After that, I went to the living room, sat close to Emma, and told her what I did.

To help others. To tell the truth. That's what really matters

.

Loneliness and Depression

My name is Amanda. I've been a Certified Nursing Assistant for ten years and love the work. When I was asked to write a short story about a lonely older person, I immediately thought about Donna.

Donna lived alone, had never been married, and outlived all her immediate family. She was thin and pale, slumped over, and used a walker. Her gray air was a tangled mess; it looked like an old bird's nest on top. The first time she reached out to take my hand, I saw caked dirt beneath her fingernails, and her hand felt like ice.

Her home was cluttered, had a musty odor, and felt like a tomb. The kitchen and bathroom were filthy. After three weeks of working hard to clean up her house, do her laundry, cook, helping her bathe, shampooing, and conditioning her tangled hair, I was ready to quit and request another client. Donna rarely uttered a word to me, and when she smiled, it seemed fake. At times, I thought her heart was as cold as her hands. The job didn't feel satisfying for me.

Finally, I decided to request another job, but I didn't want to go until my agency found a replacement. And, I felt I needed to be the one to tell Donna that I would be leaving.

Then, something happened on my fourth week there. It happened to both of us.

It was the morning that I decided to tell Donna I wouldn't be working for her anymore.

After she ate her breakfast, we sat on the couch in the living room. I glanced around the room; it looked clean

44

and comfortable. I was proud of the work I'd done. Then, I looked at her. She had styled her hair into a pretty bun on top of her head. A twinge of guilt took me by surprise. I needed to be tough and tell her I was leaving before I changed my mind and regretted it later.

"Donna, ..." I paused to control my emotions. "As soon as my agency finds a replacement for me, I'll be leaving. I do care about you, but –"

She interrupted me. "I wish you would stay. It has been a long time since someone helped me and cared for me the way you do."

She reached over, took my hand, and wrapped her hands around mine. Her hands felt soft and warm. Then she broke into a smile that seemed to light up the whole room.

I blinked away the tears from my eyes and smiled back at her.

We had connected.

I stayed with Donna for two more years and enjoyed each day with her. I was holding her hand when she died.

A Stroke

I had been working for four years with Claire, and every day was a new adventure. She was always trying to live life to the fullest and constantly joking around. I honestly enjoyed every day that I worked with her. Though the day she had a stroke was one of the most stressful times of my career, and it all started normally.

I walked in like I do every Monday morning, but Claire wasn't there to greet me as always. I was immediately concerned.

"Claire?! Claire, where are you?" I yelled into the empty room. I ran into each room until I found her lying still in her bed. "What's wrong?"

"Don't worry about me. I just don't feel good, that's all," she whispered faintly.

"Claire, what happened?"

"Well, I woke up this morning, and I wasn't feeling myself. I had a headache, blurred vision, my right arm is weak, and I felt …" her words trailed off and on again. She continued to speak, but her words slurred.

I breathed slow to calm myself and searched my mind for an answer to her problem. Then I found it. It was Donna Wilson's CNA class where we had learned about strokes from the American Stroke Association. Act F.A.S.T. – I immediately picked up Claire's phone and dialed 911.

"Claire!" I said, raising my voice, almost yelling. "We need to get you to a hospital now. An ambulance is on the way. I just called 911!"

The next thing I knew, we were in the hospital, and I was waiting for my supervisor to call me back. Claire had

47

finished all the tests and was in a hospital bed next to my chair. She had an IV dripping in her arm, using oxygen, and sleeping soundly. My hands were sweating, and my heart was beating fast. Claire was important to me. We had been through thick and thin, and she is the reason I wake up excited to go to work.

Her doctor walked in and interrupted my thoughts.

"Well, the good news is Claire is now stable from a stroke."

"What does that mean?" I questioned.

"It means she is going to live in a nursing home," a voice disrupted the doctor. A small woman was walking through the door holding her phone to her ear.

"Excuse me, who are you?" I asked with a little more force than I intended.

"I'm her niece, and I am making the call to put her in one of the local nursing homes."

"Claire told me she never wanted to go live in a nursing home," I blurted out.

"But I have medical power of attorney, so I get to decide."

It was as if her words were a weapon that speared my heart. While I felt like Claire was my family, I knew that it wasn't true, so I couldn't do anything about this. I wanted so badly for Claire to get up right then and put this awful woman in her place, but it didn't happen. I stared at the bed hoping she might sit up any minute now, but this wasn't a movie. Nothing can be that easy.

A week later, I went to the nursing home to visit Claire.

"Oh, my goodness! Is that who I think it is?" I heard the voice echoing down the hall.

I turned and smiled meeting Claire's eyes. "Yes, ma'am it is."

"Well come over and give me a hug young lady."

I hurried down the hall and hugged her tight. "It's so good to see you," I whispered.

"You too, honey. How have you been?"

"Fine. What about you?"

"Oh, you know me; I always try to look on the bright side of things."

I looked at her, and something came over me. I felt so guilty and sad that she was in a nursing home. I started sobbing.

"I know this isn't where you wanted to live, and I'm sorry."

"Oh, honey, don't cry. The folks here are caring and nice. And I've already made some new friends." She moved her right arm up and down and lifted her right foot off the floor. "Look, they are helping me recover from the stroke. Trust me; it's okay that I'm here. I like it."

She looked at me wiping away my tears. "I have you to thank for saving my life. You knew what was going on and called the ambulance. You not only saved my life, but you made my life better, and I like to think I made your life better too."

"Of course, you did, and I thank you," I said, then I smiled.

Eva and Arthritis

I am 75 years old. My name is Eva. When I retired ten years ago, I felt carefree and ready to start a new life. I'd gained 50 pounds, so I made plans to lose weight, work in the yard, plant a vegetable garden, learn to play the piano, and watch movies on Netflix. Then it happened.

At first, I blamed my early morning aches and pains on the frequent change of the weather. Then I started experiencing a lot of pain in my knees and lower back. At

51

times it felt like someone had stabbed me in the back with a sharp knife and twisted it. After that, my hands started getting stiff and sore. I consciously moved them during the day, and that helped get rid of some of the stiffness. Later, little lumps and bumps started popping up on my finger joints; they hurt when I touched them. Cooking became a challenge, so I signed up for Meals on Wheels. I'm grateful for that wonderful service. It gave me a sense of connection with the outside world and brought me good meals.

Within a month, I was tired all the time. The pain in my back started shooting down my right leg. I tried every homemade remedy I read on the internet, but nothing worked. The pain in my right knee became too much to cope with, so I bought a cane. It helped take off some of the pressure when I walked.

Looking back, I'm sure I was in denial. I knew what was wrong with me. I watched my mother and my aunts suffer and become debilitated with arthritis.

I read on the Arthritis Foundation's website that arthritis is the most common cause of disability in our country, and it was my worst enemy. My joints felt angry and decaying. I needed a branch of hope, something, or someone to hold onto, but my only child lived miles away. The next day, I made an appointment to see my doctor.

My doctor is the one who helped me. He did x-rays and confirmed my greatest fear. I had generalized debilitating joint disease, osteoarthritis. He told me it was the "wear and tear" arthritis that involves the destruction of the cartilage, the cushion or shock absorber on the ends of the bones. He ordered physical therapy, an anti-inflammatory, and suggested a private care agency evaluate me for their services for personal care and housekeeping. He encouraged me; he was the branch of hope I had needed.

Thank goodness, it only took a few days for the medicine to help. I started physical therapy treatments, and I'm now feeling a little better. A nurse from Mattie's Home Care is scheduled to see me tomorrow. I'm looking forward to that visit.

This morning, I thought about my wonderful mother. Although she had to use a wheelchair because of arthritis, she never complained. I don't want to end up in a wheelchair, but I do want to be more like my mother. She was a strong woman. She told me many times that wherever there is life, there is hope.

Death and Dying

My name is Nancy. I've never married, and I live alone. After losing my parents at a young age, my grandmother raised me. She was the best grandmother in the world. I loved her very much. She was a hard worker, loving, fun, kind, and full of wisdom. She had a special way of pouring her unconditional love into everything she did, from cooking to disciplining me.

When my grandmother died, my heart broke. I lost interest in life and quit my job as a waitress. After weeks of grieving and hurting, my best friend told me I needed a purpose in my life, so I became a Home Care Aide.

My first assignment was taking care of Rachael. She was 88 years old and recently had a stroke. Her left arm was paralyzed, and she had slurred speech. She understood everything but rarely tried to talk.

She needed 24-hour care. Her family stayed with her in the evenings and nights. The agency I worked for provided care during the day. I was her main aide.

The first time I saw Rachael, my heart pounded in my chest. She looked like my grandmother. I think she saw the shocked look on my face before I could hide it because she reached out her right hand to me and smiled.

I took her hand. It felt soft and warm, like my grandmother's hand. From that moment on, I knew I had once again found purpose in my life.

During my orientation, one of the office staff told

me not to get my feelings and heart involved in my job—I'm glad that's not a rule.

I immediately felt close to Rachael and her family, and I gave her excellent care. Every day was a joy to be with her. We did fun things for her rehabilitation: cooked together, played the piano together using one hand, worked on her balance by slow dancing to her favorite music, and I often read to her, mainly the poetry she loved.

One year later, Rachael had another stroke and died. Once again, I felt the painful emotions that come when someone you love dies.

The family knew how much I cared for their mother, so they invited me to sit with them during the funeral to celebrate and honor Rachael's life. After the funeral, I was never in touch with them.

Years from now, I doubt if they will remember my name, but I believe they will remember what I did for Rachael and them.

Aging

S he stood in awe as a beautiful rainbow spread across the celestial-blue sky. The fresh scent of rain lingered in the air. It fed her soul and lifted her spirits. But when she turned around to go inside, she saw her reflection in the sliding glass door and sighed: *If only I could look as young and good as I feel now.*

And so she began a personal journey to look as

young and good as she felt. She hobbled inside to the bathroom and gazed in the mirror.

"Oh my! I looked withered and washed out. I've got to do something about it!"

Coveting a new look, she shuffled to her computer and searched for beauty experts.

She spent $129.99 on natural herbal creams to tighten her saggy face. For an additional $29.95, she ordered a secret anti-aging paste with a miraculous formula in a full coverage foundation that eliminated wrinkles. She ordered a pair of dark-brown, extra-long human hair eyelashes, and a new premium-quality wig; all on sale with free shipping.

Three days later, after the packages arrived, she went into the bedroom, sat in front of the dresser mirror, trimmed and plucked out her gray, wiry eyebrows, drew on some dark eyeliner, and applied the fake eyelashes on her acorn-shaped eyes. She put on her new bouffant wig, her favorite purple dress, fake pearl necklace, and matching earrings. Last, but not least, she opened the new, revolutionary skin products. With the inspiration of a talented sculptor, she shaped, molded, and shaded her asymmetrical face with the new miracle products.

After the transformation was complete, she was exhausted. She shuffled to her favorite rocking chair, sat down, and gently rocked back and forth, back and forth.

Suddenly, she heard footsteps. She threw back her shoulders.

It was him! The love of her life. Her husband of 51 years.

The doorknob turned. Her heart thumped loudly in her chest, and her breath quickened.

The door opened wide.

His jaw dropped.

"Do you think I look pretty?" she asked with pride.

"I think you look pretty…. ridiculous," he quickly replied. "True beauty comes from the soul. Just be yourself!"

Nutrition and Ms. Sofia

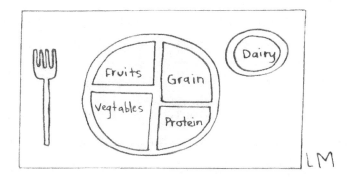

LM

When I was first introduced to Ms. Sofia, I was incredibly overwhelmed. I walked into her house and could tell that I had my work cut out for me. Her primary diagnosis was undernutrition caused by a poor diet. While Ms. Sofia was a kind woman, she had altogether stopped taking care of herself. Her hair was dull, and her face gaunt and slightly gray. Her clothes hung off her body, concealing her frail body. She was 80 years old, and her only companion was a cat. She had a limited income and spent a lot of it on the cat, so there wasn't much left for herself.

"Hello, my name is Annabelle. How are you?" I smiled at her, trying to hide the real concern that was in my eyes.

"To be honest, I feel tired and cold all the time." She garbled some of her words because she had lost most of her teeth. "I'm not sure I'll get better, and in my opinion, this aging thing is pretty tough."

Her kitchen was dirty, and the food cabinet and refrigerator were almost bare. Meals on Wheels containers were littered everywhere. However, she did tell me how Meals on Wheels is her sunshine in the rain. She enjoys talking to the friendly people who bring her meals. While they come routinely, she can't eat some of their food because of her missing teeth, and the amount she eats isn't enough to keep her healthy. That's only a part of Ms. Sofia's problems. Another problem is that she never goes to the grocery store, and her friend who did take her passed away last year. I knew that if I wanted to help Ms. Sofia stay at home as she wanted, I had to help her make some drastic changes.

First, I needed to help her eat properly. I found her hand grinder in her cabinet, and she started grinding some of the foods she liked, but couldn't chew, from Meals on Wheels. When I was learning about nutrition in school, ChooseMyPlate.gov was a site that all my teachers encouraged me to use. I decided that it would be a good idea to try to teach Ms. Sofia about this plate. We printed a copy and taped it on the front of her fridge.

"Look, Ms. Sofia, your plate needs to be filled with almost half of the vegetables, and a large portion of fruit as well. Then grains and protein need to be about a fourth of your plate, and off to the side a small portion of dairy." I explained the diagram to her, and she nodded in agreement and repeated the portions to me without looking at the plate. But then I realized something; she needed help to access good food.

Now, this was the most difficult task, but I taught her how to order her healthy groceries, and less expensive cat food, online with a small laptop computer that her neighbor gave her before she died. Ms. Sofia seemed to be enjoying learning all these new ways to help herself, but I knew she couldn't do it alone. So, I promised her that I would be there every step of the way.

About two months later, I walked in one morning, and the smell of fresh breakfast filled the house. I saw Ms. Sofia sitting at the table happily enjoying what looked like a perfect portioned plate. She motioned for me to sit down.

After I sat, she looked into my eyes. "Listen, Annabelle; I just wanted to thank you for all your help. I feel good, and I've gained weight. I don't think I would have made it without your help. I was truly hopeless until you came along."

"Ms. Sofia, I don't know what to say." I started to tear up.

"You don't have to say anything. Just look at this." She smiled, looking at her homemade breakfast.

"Okay!" I laughed, feeling accomplished.

Eccentric and Entertaining

My name is Diana, and I'm a retired Home Health Care Aide. I worked for a hospital-based agency for twenty-five years. Although it was demanding physical work, to me, it was a labor of love. I believed my presence, and the tasks I did, truly made a positive difference in a person's life. And even though I encountered some strange patients and stressful situations in the homes, most visits were interesting and gratifying. There was one eccentric patient who was my favorite. The year was 1984, and her name was Sally Allen.

Sally was eighty years old. She had diabetes with a recent right leg amputation below her knee. She lived alone with no running water or electricity and lived on a monthly income of $260.00, plus food stamps. Her only relative was a nephew who lived out of state. I was assigned to her to assist with her personal care and household tasks.

Excited about my new assignment, I remember placing the referral on my clipboard, smiling, and telling the admitted nurse goodbye. A few minutes later, I started on a home health visit that would take me back in time without a wormhole or swirling lights and tunnels, but with the most enjoyable and entertaining patient I'd ever met.

Everywhere I looked, the autumn leaves on the trees were bursting with gorgeous-red, gleaming-gold, and bright-orange fall colors. I followed the directions on the referral, and twenty minutes later turned north on old Highway 43. I drove to the edge of the small town of Hartsville and traveled three miles south on a dirt road. Next, I veered right onto an even worse dirt road, the twisting and bumpy road to meet Sally Allen.

I drove exactly two more miles until I came to Sally Allen's mailbox. I stopped my car behind the mailbox, glanced across a pasture, and saw an old wooden house surrounded by a barbed wire fence.

When I got out of my car, I saw a gray-headed woman sitting on the porch in a wheelchair. She was waving her hand, beckoning me forward. I decided to leave my car near the mailbox and walk to the house. As I walked up the dirt road toward the house, on my left, behind the barbed wire fence, an old sway-back brown horse lifted his head and glanced toward me as if to say, "welcome."

The front yard was overgrown with weeds. The ramshackle house had wooden siding warped with age. The roof on the front porch sagged. I carefully stepped up onto the porch, smiled, and said, "Hello, my name is Diana. I'm a home health aide, and I work with Racheal, the nurse that was here yesterday. I've come to help you."

She looked at me with dark brown eyes that had a penetrating quality. Few patients I visited looked me directly in the eyes like she did. Suddenly, she looked away. There was complete silence. She must be shy, or so I thought.

The silence lengthened until she finally said, "Looks like you've come to the right place." Her voice sounded much younger than she looked; it was clear and radiant. "Call me Sally. I'm a bachelor girl, not an old maid, and I own this farm. I've lived here all my life. I call my farm Peace in the Valley, Alaska in the Winter, and Hell in the Summer." From that moment on, I knew she wasn't shy.

After she told me she planned to build a porch ramp so she could do her outside chores, she quizzed me about my qualifications and personal information. For example, she asked, "Do you have a family?"

"Yes," I replied.

"Do you love them?"

"With all my heart," I said.

"I'm glad you didn't say you love them with all of your brain. That's the part that gets confused sometimes."

I smiled and nodded my head. She invited me inside and shoved the front door open with her foot.

Everything looked clean, comfortable, and old. It

felt like I had stepped 100 years back in time. The living room, kitchen, and bedroom were in one large open area with a stone fireplace on one side. The room was furnished with a rocking chair, an old pump organ with ornate carvings on the front, a small wooden table, two cane-back straight chairs, an old oak dresser with a large mirror, and a kitchen cabinet with a hand water pump attached to the sink. A large kerosene stove sat next to a bed covered with a pretty khaki and beige patchwork quilt, and beige curtains hung on the front windows.

She rolled Silver, the name she had given her wheelchair, up to the table. "You're invited to sit at the table with Silver and me."

"I'm honored, thank you."

"And I thank you. I wasn't allowed to sit at the table with my family." She lowered her voice, almost to a whisper, and I remember every word. "My mother hated me and didn't let me go to school. She made me stay home and do all the work. My sister taught me how to read and write. She's the one who told me that I'm an incest child. When I asked my mother if it was true, she said yes. Then, she beat my sister to a pulp for telling me the truth."

I made eye contact with her. She had the appearance of someone at peace, and I believed her. I reached across the small table, and she took my hand. We sat hand-in-hand until she broke the silence.

"Well, I survived and outlived all of them. I have one nephew who lives on the other side of the state. He'll inherit my farm." She let go of my hand. Her eyes began to sparkle as she told me more about her life. "Once a week I pay my neighbors to feed my horse and wild critters. They also bring me an ice chest filled with food and drinking water and leave it on the porch for me."

I listened to one story after another and began to see the world through Sally's eyes. She loved animals, music, angels, holidays, and cooking holiday meals. Her only meal guest was Carl, her long-haired yellow cat who had a strange meow and looked like he'd just been in a fight. She especially loved Christmas and would decorate her home and sing Christmas songs to Carl.

After she finished talking, I assisted her with a sponge bath and did the other household chores listed on her Care Plan. She didn't want me to fix her lunch because she enjoyed doing that.

Before I left, she wanted to sing for me and see if she could play the pump organ with one leg. Of course, I said yes.

She rolled Silver to the organ and pumped the wooden foot pedal hard with one leg, and music filled the room. Her voice was mellow and beautiful as if she was born to sing. After she sang the final note of "I'll Fly Away," I clapped and clapped. She twirled around on the organ stool, smiled, and gracefully bowed as if she was on stage.

I looked at my watch and was surprised by how long I'd been there. I left Sally's home that day with a smile on my face and loving home health even more than the day before.

That weekend, her neighbor built her a wooden ramp on her front porch. He built sturdy handrails on both sides and made it wide enough for her wheelchair.

On my next visit, after I finished my assigned duties, Sally told me she had something important to ask me before I had to go. We sat on the porch, enjoying the gentle heat. She closed her eyes, turned her face toward the sun, reached up her hands past the top of her head, and wiggled her fingers in the air like a child. Then she placed her hands in her lap, opened her eyes, and said, "Tell me about Guardian Angels."

"I know that Guardian Angels are supposed to protect and guide us in life," I replied.

"Knowing and feeling are two different things. The difference between knowing something and feeling something is that when you feel something you use your heart, and your heart helps you learn what your mind already knows, and that can make it real to you."

By the time Sally finished talking, small gusts of wind had blown in. Goosebumps popped up on arms, and a chill went up my spine and traveled to the top of my head.

I enjoyed each visit and listened and learned. Here are some other things Sally taught me: How to fluff and make a feather bed properly. The correct way to empty slop outside and how to fill a kerosene stove and cook on it. How, and where, to feed wild wolves. Ways to celebrate life and holidays with private, festive occasions. And how to get rid of pain by singing an uplifting song.

As her surgical wound healed, Sally gained strength and did most of the "chores" she did before the amputation.

She refused to accept another agency to come to her home and help her with personal care, shopping, and housekeeping. When I was on my last official visit with her, she gave me her neighbor's phone number so I could call him if I needed to give her a message.

I knew she had to be discharged from home health, but I couldn't discharge her from my life.

Two days before Christmas, I went to visit Sally. She was happy and doing well. Sparkly red and green Christmas tinsel decorated the inside of her home. We sat at the table with Carl the Cat and had our own special, delicious Christmas meal. After eating, she told me her brief version of the original Christmas story, and then we sang Christmas songs as she played her pump organ.

When I hugged her good-bye, she surprised me with the perfect Christmas gift by saying, "I love you."

"I love you too," I said with tears clouding my eyes.

Two weeks later, we had the heaviest snowfall seen in years. It was gorgeous — a perfectly white wonderland. But after the snow, a damaging ice storm hit. It crippled the upper half of the state, including where we lived. Stranded cars were on the highways, power lines were down, and schools and stores were closed. Our home was without electricity for two days, but the phone lines still worked.

I called Sally's neighbor to check up on her, but their phone was out of order, so I called the Hartsville Police Department. I told the man who answered the phone about Sally, and he knew where she lived. He assured me they would check on her and get back to me.

Later that day, a lady from the police department called me and said they found Sally in bed. Her kerosene stove was off. She had signs of frostbite, and her left leg looked gangrenous. She was weak but able to talk. They transported her to the hospital where she was admitted.

As soon as the roads were safe for travel, I drove to the hospital. When I inquired about Sally's condition, the nurse told me Sally was terminal, and she had requested Hospice.

I knew Sally was at the end of life when I saw her. She was gasping for air, and her hands were a mottled bluish-purple. However, she opened her eyes when she heard my voice, and we held hands like the first day I had met her.

"This place is full of woodrats. Please stay with

me."

My eyes filled with tears. "I'd be honored to stay with you," I said.

I sat by her bedside, still holding her hand. Thirty minutes later, Sally peacefully took her last breath.

I met Sally's nephew at her funeral. There were four there: Her nephew, her neighbor, my husband, and I.

At Sally's request, she was buried next to her mother.

Cancer

B reast cancer is a scary diagnosis to face, and it also has a huge impact on the families of the victims. This disease runs in my family. My grandmother, two of my aunts, and my mom have all had it. Sadly, my grandmother and aunts died.

My mom survived. She is the most positive, strong-willed, and overall amazing person I have ever known. A diagnosis of breast cancer used to be a death sentence in my grandmother's days. While the technology and advancements in today's medicine have allowed for more people to survive cancer, it is still a very difficult process to go through. My mom may have survived, but I still get scared when she isn't feeling well.

Cancer can deeply affect a family, and that's why I almost didn't accept Mrs. Lilah as a client.

Mrs. Lilah is 72 years old with a diagnosis of recurrent breast cancer. She had a mastectomy 12 years ago, but now the cancer was back and had spread to her bones. This particular job just hit too close to home, but the agency didn't have any more openings. I needed the money, so I accepted the job.

Within the first week, I had already made a connection with Mrs. Lilah, and we bonded. My job consisted of assisting with meals, housekeeping, and personal care, but I mostly enjoyed all the stories she told me. She was an avid storyteller. She could bring a simple idea to life with just her words. She was also an exceptional artist. I loved looking at her art. You could see the transitions of life she went through in her paintings.

Over the next couple of weeks, Mrs. Lilah became weaker and had more pain. I was worried about what might happen. I even thought about asking to be transferred to another case. But she was the one with a tough decision to make. Would she continue to fight it? Or stop all the chemotherapy and risk not getting better? I could tell the cancer treatments were taking a toll on her. Then one day she told me what she was going to do, and why.

"For a long time, I didn't think I had much left to fight for, but ever since you came into my life, I have had a reason to fight back."

"Wait does that mean--"

She cut me off before I could even finish my sentence. "Yes. I am going to continue with the treatments."

I pulled her into a hug, and I could feel the tears starting to fall from my eyes. I couldn't lose another person to cancer. I cared deeply for her.

We stopped hugging and walked to her art studio, where a new piece was sitting on the table. It was a silhouette drawing of a woman who looked like me. It was me!

"You inspired me to keep living and fighting. You gave me hope," she said.

Pneumonia

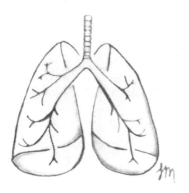

After working with clients, it becomes very easy to get attached and build strong, healthy relationships with them. This happens a lot, and in no way is a bad thing, but it makes it harder when they have health problems. I have had multiple clients over the years, but there's one who touched my life more than the others.

Her name is Hazel. She is 91 years old, small, and frail. She is also one of the most delightful people I have ever met, and I love working with her. She's older and more susceptible to illnesses, but she insisted on going with me to one day to get her groceries, so I said yes.

We got everything on her list except her prescriptions. As we headed toward the pharmacy to pick them up, I noticed that quite a few customers were coughing and sneezing.

Then I saw the sign. HAVE YOU HAD YOUR FLU AND PNEUMONIA VACCINES? *Oh my, why did I bring her with me?*

I think she saw the distraught look on my face.

"Stop your worrying. I'm going to be fine, and I'm having a good time."

A few days later, Hazel seemed more tired than usual and had a nasty cough. I was concerned, but she reassured me it was only a cold. About three hours later, when I was about to leave, I noticed her face looked flushed. Her forehead was hot to touch, and she started shaking like she was chilling. I quickly took her temperature. It was 100 degrees.

"I'm having a little trouble getting some air," she

said between short, quick breaths. She pointed to her chest. "And there's a sharp pain, here, when I take in a breath."

My heart raced, but I tried to stay calm. I called my supervisor and explained the situation. She told me since Hazel was having trouble breathing and pains when she breathed that I needed to call 911, and she would notify Hazel's relatives.

By the time the ambulance had arrived, Hazel was having more trouble breathing, and her temperature spiked to 102 degrees.

I watched as the flashing lights and blaring sirens disappeared into the distance. After I calmed down, I drove to the agency to talk to Rachael, the R.N. Supervisor, blaming myself all the way there for what happened to Hazel.

"Rachael, I shouldn't have taken Hazel shopping. I feel like it's my fault she got sick."

"I just got off the phone with her daughter, and she told me that Hazel's condition is stable. She has pneumonia, and they'll admit her to the hospital. She said Hazel had a flu shot and the pneumonia vaccine." She handed me an article titled *Pneumonia and the Elderly.*

"This article will help you understand."

I thanked her.

"You're welcome. Hazel's daughter said that you're her mother's favorite aide, and she has had a different one each year since the age of 80."

I looked down at the pages in my hands, and then my tears started to hit the white paper. It was making marks, so I looked back up at Rachael. She had a comforting look on her face. She hugged me and told me I should see Hazel tomorrow, but I needed to take care of myself tonight and get some rest.

The next morning, I went to the hospital to see Hazel. I knocked softly on the door, walked into her room, and saw her in bed. She turned to face me and smiled.

"Well, I was wondering when you were going to come."

"Here I am," I said quietly and sat down in the chair next to her bed. "I'm sorry you got pneumonia."

"Honey, you saved my life. I'm old, and sickness is going to get me sometimes, but it didn't this time thanks to you. I heard my mama's country doctor tell her that pneumonia is an old person's friend, and I'm not quite ready for that lasting friendship."

I smiled.

Hazel took my hand and squeezed it.

I'm so grateful she is sitting beside me today.

Self-Care

I started working as an aide because I love helping people and want to be a nurse one day. But it was only recently that I realized that it is also important to take care of myself too.

It has been about three years since I started as an aide, and sometimes it feels like I can't do it. I have two clients that I care about very much, but they take up a lot of my energy. I also have two kids and am a single mother. Sometimes, I feel the odds are stacked against me, and with each passing day, I get more tired.

My morning starts by going to Ms. Gracie's house. She is a widow and a diabetic. She requires a lot of attention since she had to have her foot amputated last year due to her disease. I give her my absolute all. She tells me every day before I leave that I am the reason she is still fighting. I could never leave her.

Then my afternoon is filled up by taking care of a Vietnam veteran, Mr. Claud. He is a nice man but has had a lot of physical problems and PTSD. His wife, Nancy, tells me he still questions why his friends died during battle, but he survived.

Nancy takes good care of him, as much as she can, but she is on oxygen all day, so I work hard to help them. Most days, I wish I could do more.

After work, I come home to my little girl, Olive, and son, Jacob. They are good kids, but ever since the divorce, there has been some unspoken tension in the house. Jacob is upset with me that I left their dad, but they aren't old enough yet to understand what happened to us.

When I was a little girl, I saw my life very differently, but I am doing what I love, so I need to figure out a way to continue, but still be happy. I had been struggling for weeks when Ms. Gracie noticed something wasn't right.

I came in one morning after a particularly stressful night, and Ms. Gracie was sitting in the living room. She motioned for me to sit next to her, so I went over.

"Good morning Ms. Gracie. How are you doing?" I asked, holding back a yawn.

"I'm not dumb."

"What? I don't understand."

"Don't give me this fake conversation. What is going on with you? You haven't been yourself lately. At first, I thought it was just a funk, but now I am worried about you."

"My agency doesn't want their employees talking about their problems with the clients."

"Hellooo…I have known you for three years, and I can tell when something is wrong. I don't want details, just the big picture. What is it?"

"I have just been stressed. My life is a little more chaotic than I imagined it would be."

"Oh, honey, everyone gets stressed," she said, patting my shoulder and smiling from ear to ear.

"I know, but sometimes the stress starts to take over my life."

"Well, then we need to fix this."

She took my hand and led me to the back of her house, where she had her office. It was full of books. She had been a teacher, so she collected all sorts of books. She reached for a tall, thick book in the corner and handed it to me. "I want you to borrow this book." The title read, *How to De-stress your Life.*

"What is this?" I asked as I started to examine the book.

"This is something my husband gave me right after I had my first child. I had been working like crazy and started to feel overwhelmed with worry about the baby. So, he got me this, and it changed my life. There are all kinds of different techniques to help you."

I just looked at her and smiled. She brought me in

for a hug and held me tight. I couldn't wait to go home and read the book.

After I had finally tucked the kids into bed, I went downstairs, and there on my kitchen table was the book. I sat down and opened it. I started reading and was amazed at how many ways someone could de-stress their lives. I looked up at the clock, and it was one in the morning. I almost finished the whole book. I was so excited.

Over the next couple of weeks, I started to implement things the book recommended doing. I made to-do lists to organize myself, drank calming green tea, and meditated before bed. I also took walks with my kids to help get the blood pumping and took salt baths on the weekends.

I started focusing some time on myself, and it made my life so much happier. Then, in turn, I could help those around me even more.

Diabetic Neuropathy

S ame old, same old. Get the coffee ready to brew the night before. Wake up to an empty house, stumble to the kitchen, turn on the coffee pot and think about her while waiting on my first cup of morning coffee.

Since my wife died three years ago, I'd been spending my days watching my life go by. My daughter told me I acted depressed, begged me to go to the doctor, and borderline nagged me to take care of myself because of my diabetes.

My name is David Newman, and I'm 76 years old.

Last year, my feet started feeling numb at times during the day, then the rest of the time they tingled and burned. It was worse at nights with a pin-prickling feeling with sharp, stabbing pains. The pain never went away. I felt like my feet weren't touching the ground when I walked, and I fell a few times.

One evening, I dropped a glass in the kitchen. It broke and spattered all over the floor, so I swept it up and went to bed.

Next morning, same old, same old, except I forgot about the broken glass and went to the kitchen barefooted. Although I didn't feel anything happen to my feet, I must have stepped on a piece of glass because I saw blood on the floor. The bleeding soon stopped. I didn't feel any glass in the bottom of my feet, so I wiped up the blood and showered.

The following week, my daughter came over to help me around the house and cut my toenails. When she lifted my right foot, she discovered an open sore on the bottom of my foot. She said it looked like a red crater with pus at the bottom of it, so she cleaned it and covered it with a bandage. The following day, she took me to the doctor.

I told my doctor about the numbness and pain in my feet. He said he was certain I had Diabetic Peripheral Neuropathy. He explained the condition to me, looked at my foot and cleaned it, then put a dressing on it. He told me to stay off of it as much as possible, gave me a prescription for antibiotics, and ordered Home Health for wound care.

I liked the R.N. from the home health agency. Her name was Debbie Evans. During her visits, she taught me a lot. She explained that peripheral means bordering or outlying, beyond the brain and spinal cord. Neuro means related to the nerves, and pathy means disease. Together it refers to a condition where the nerves that carry messages from the brain and spinal cord to the rest of the body are damaged or diseased. She told me the nerves must have a reason for being damaged or diseased, and the cause for my nerve damage was diabetes. Since my father and his mother had diabetes, my neuropathy was inherited. I learned that there is no cure for hereditary neuropathy, but that's not the case for other types of neuropathy.

Debbie taught me the importance of preventing

blood sugar spikes and encouraged me to stay on my diet.

She stated in words that I could understand. She said that over time increased blood sugar levels cause the vessels that supply the nerves to become constricted or narrowed. That can cause damage to the nerves. High blood sugar levels also may attack the myelin that surrounds the nerves. Myelin is the sheath that forms around nerves, including those in the brain and spinal cord. It allows impulses to transmit quickly, and efficiently, along the nerve cells.

If anyone reading this story has diabetes, please do everything you can to prevent blood sugar spikes. I'm sure you know the drill.

Debbie helped me understand my condition, and she took good care of my foot wound, but it still wasn't healing. She called my doctor, and that afternoon I was back in his office.

My doctor sent me to the wound center. My daughter took me there every day for a week, but the wound kept getting worse. I could smell a foul odor coming from it. Gradually, my entire foot was pale; then it turned a darker color. They did some tests and told me I had gangrene in my foot.

I was in the hospital when the decision was made to amputate my foot to keep the gangrene from spreading.

I didn't want to be a burden to my family, so I admitted myself to the New Hope Nursing Center. I'm writing my story at my bedside table, relaxed, and sitting up in my bed.

It's not the same old, same old here. There's something for us residents to do all day long. Everyone works hard here, and everyone is kind to me. I especially like the CNAs. (Certified Nursing Assistants)

A nurse checks my blood sugar routinely and gives me my insulin shot. I go to the dining room and eat tasty and balanced meals. I go to church every Sunday, and I've made some good friends. The doctor ordered Physical Therapy for me, so I'm getting stronger every day and learning to walk with an artificial foot.

I'm glad I'm here.

I've also met a fine woman across the hall in room 104; she reminds me of my wife.

Pain

Trigeminal Neuralgia is nerve pain that affects the 5th cranial nerve, the trigeminal nerve, that carries sensation from your face to your brain. Trigeminal Neuralgia, also known as tic douloureux, is triggered by things such as brushing your teeth, washing your face, shaving, chewing, or putting on makeup. Even a light breeze against your face might set off the pain. The pain usually affects only one side of the face and can be caused by several disorders.

An abscessed tooth caused his trigeminal neuralgia. When they removed the tooth, he felt immediate relief.

Unbearable, excruciating, and torturous are the words he used to describe his pain. Others have described it as the most unbearable pain known to humanity.

He was 93 years old. He'd been shot, had sprains and strains, joint replacements, and broken bones. He knew pain.

One morning, when he was brushing his teeth, an attack of unbearable pain hit the right side of his face. He clenched his jaws and grabbed the edge of the sink to keep from falling. A few seconds later, it left. When his home care aide came on duty, he told the aide about his excruciating pain.

The aide asked him if it felt like he had a bad toothache.

He answered yes and said he needed a good shave before he went to the dentist. The aide used an electric razor but had to stop before finishing the job; the man had another attack of pain. He described it as torturous.

The man knew pain. He was a World War II Veteran.

A Tribute to World War II Veterans
and To All of Those Who Know

There are those who know

Listen to them and look into their eyes

They understand true courage, duty, and the pain of sacrifice

Wrapped in innocence, they journeyed into darkness, not knowing if it would take their life

They put service before self so future generations wouldn't have to take the same, perilous path

Years may dim memories, but not their valor and their deeds for you and me

Listen to them, look into their eyes, they all know the price to pay for being free

There are those who asked that their life not be saved, but that they may be calm to complete their assigned duties and save others that day

There are those who know what hunger and starvation looks like, and how it feels to move lifeless soldiers off the battlefield

Look into the eyes of those who know how the green grass turned blood red

And then tell others who don't know

Tell them to look at the stars and stripes, and listen to those who know

Then give thanks, and say thank you, to all of those who know

My Rights

LM

Encapsulated in her queenly cocoon of self, her hands tight upon the armrests of her royal blue electric recliner, I could tell Mrs. Katrina Khan was going to bellow out another order before it was time for me to leave.

I'd only worked there one-week, and I kept my mouth shut as I listened to her bark orders at me, one after another, all week. I worked hard trying to please her, but she never had a kind word for me, and she called me "Hey Girl."

"Hey Girl, Princess Poodle just pooped on the living room floor," she said with a smirk on her face. "Would you please clean that up for me before you leave for the day."

"No, ma'am. I can't. Don't you remember that Jennifer, the nurse, told you that I'm not allowed to clean up your pet's poop?"

She shook her finger at me; her fiery, red finger polish flashed in the air. Her eyes narrowed to a squint.

I wasn't prepared for what happened next.

She got out of her recliner with the speed of someone 20 years younger and kicked her walker to the floor. She lied. She didn't need a walker like she had me and everyone else believe.

Before I realized it, she was standing in front of me. Then she got in my face. Her wheezy, cackling voice rose

99

higher and higher. Words hurled from her mouth, "You're here to work for me, not to question my authority!"

"Yes, ma'am."

I turned around and quietly and quickly opened the front door and walked out. I stopped at a nearby park and wrote down every detail of what happened that day in Mrs. Khan's home. Then, I drove to my agency and gave my report to my supervisor. After reading about the incident, she informed me that I made the right decision to leave. She said she would make a home visit to talk to Mrs. Khan. She also stated this was the second incident reported by an employee that Mrs. Khan had violated their rights as an aide.

Aides Have the Right to:

Work in a safe environment.

Be treated without discrimination.

Be free from harassment, abuse, attack, verbal, and mental abuse.

Not be abused by any means (e.g., verbal, emotional, physical, sexual, or financial).

Receive considerate and respectful behavior from clients and patients.

Protect themselves from physical attack.

Not put their lives, their physical health, or the health of their families at risk.

Have reasonable access to the tools needed to perform the duties of their position.

Be given enough personal time during the work shift to keep hydrated and nourished as needed.

Receive timely payment for services provided, including wages, expenditures made on behalf of clients, and expenditures resulting from using their vehicles for clients.

Receive protection for whistleblowing to expose fraud and corrupt actions.

Disclose information relating to the conduct of an employer or another employee for illegal actions, criminal offenses, discrimination, environmental dangers; and health or safety dangers.

File complaints and grievances without fear of retaliation.

Be notified if complaints are registered against them; and, have the right to address registered complaints, have investigations conducted confidentially, have fair and unbiased hearings; and be given the results of the investigations.

Give input to the Care Team.

Rheumatoid Arthritis

The house is still standing where I made home health visits years ago. It has been abandoned for at least twenty years, and the yard is thickly overgrown with weeds and brush. When you drive by the house during the winter, you can see the crumbling walls, sagging porch, and shattered windows–shattered like the lives of those who lived before we had the medicines of today–medicines that inspires hopes and cures for diseases.

The home health patient who lived there suffered from debilitating Rheumatoid Arthritis (RA). I use the word *suffer* because that is how he described his crippled and painful joints. He was 52 years old, and his 47-year-old wife was his devoted caregiver. I met them on their 25th wedding anniversary, and he called her his perfect soulmate with an eternal bond. He said that every time he moaned or groaned, she jumped as if a cord tied her to his waist. I vividly remember he told me that he lived for her and would die for her.

They didn't have children but were foster parents for a few years before RA attacked him. He said he was a warrior and fought hard to conquer the disease. However, the disease won and took away most of his energy. His noble intent went with it, so he decided to accept everything and stop fighting. During the interview, he told me he had to negotiate purposeful body movements instead of automatically doing them. He suffered every day because of his painful and crippled joints.

His back was twisted and hunched over, and his hands were curved with large and boggy nodules on every finger. He had enough movement in them to hold utensils to feed himself and turn the pages in a book. Due to the severe joint deformities in his knees and feet, he couldn't stand or walk and needed a wheelchair for mobility. His wife used a mechanical lift to transfer him.

He kept a stack of books on his bedside table and spent most of his time reading. He was well-informed about his disease. He said he learned all about RA when he was fighting it like a warrior. He told me that RA is caused by the immune system attacking healthy body tissue, including joints and other body tissues. He understood that the immune system mistakenly sends antibodies to the lining of joints where they assault the tissue, causing painful swelling, bone erosion, and deformities. There are theories of why the immune system starts to attack the joints, such as an infection, virus, genetics, or the environment, but none have been proven. He was certain his RA was genetic. He had three sisters, and all of them had an autoimmune disease.

He was working full-time as an accountant when he first noticed something was wrong. It started with severe fatigue and other flu-like symptoms, but his went beyond that. He began to lose function in his hands; buttons were hard to fasten, and he frequently dropped items, such as his writing pens. Because his RA started suddenly with severe fatigue and involvement of the hands, feet, and knees, his diagnosis was made rapidly. Blood tests also confirmed the disease.

After I finished my nursing assessment, I drew his blood to take to the referring doctor's office. Before I left, he gracefully declined physical therapy services and an aide to assist with personal care. His wife agreed, and I respected their decision.

When I returned to the office, I wrote my nursing note, found our Med-Surg book, and reviewed Rheumatoid Arthritis. One paragraph caught my attention. *The difficulties that accompanies living with RA are fear, loneliness, depression, anger, and anxiety. If unacknowledged, it can be overwhelming.* I felt relieved our new patient had found acceptance and was receiving home health care.

One week later, I scheduled a follow-up visit to draw his blood for a different test. On the day of the visit, I picked a small bouquet of flowers from my yard as a late gift for their wedding anniversary.

It was a gorgeous, sunny day. As I entered their yard with the flowers in my hand, a beautiful butterfly flew past my face like a gorgeous flower flying in the air. I hurried up the steps of their front porch and rang the doorbell. Suddenly, I heard it! I knew a gunshot when I heard one. It came from the living room where he stayed. The door was unlocked, so I rushed inside as fast as I could.

He knew what he was doing. He had placed the barrel of a 45-caliber pistol to the roof of his mouth, pointed directly at his brain. By the time I reached him, blood and brain matter were on him and his bed. He was dead.

Seconds later, his wife frantically ran into the room, screaming in terror.

Adrenaline surged through my veins. I yelled at her to dial 911 for an ambulance!

I quickly positioned him flat on the bed with the intent to resuscitate him, but his mouth was shattered-- shattered like the lives of many debilitated victims who lived before we had the medicines of today—medicines that inspires hopes and cures for diseases.

Professional Communication

S ome of my friends, who are also aides, started telling stories about lessons we learned the hard way about professional communication with our clients and family members. They asked me to write them down and share them so other aides won't make the same mistakes, or, as one friend called them, "bloopers."

Lesson 1: Report a bad situation to the supervisor and don't say anything about it to the family or client.

I liked working with one of my clients, but I couldn't stand her two teenage grandsons. I was only around them once, and that was once too many. They looked dirty and smelled it too. When they visited, they ate everything they could find in the refrigerator, cursed in front of their grandmother, and called her "The Old Bag."

Before I left work that day, I decided to tell their mother how the boys treated their grandmother, so I asked to speak to her in private.

Here is what the boys' mother screamed at me:

"Get out of this house, you nosey b_ _ _ _ _, and don't let the door hit you on the way out!"

Lesson 2: Treat the client with dignity and don't use terms of endearment or nicknames.

I'm friendly, very caring, and a hard worker. When I started working as an aide, I was so excited about getting to work with the elderly. I made my spending money in high school by babysitting and thought the job would be similar.

WRONG.

I made a mistake of saying the following: "I'll be glad to help you, sweetie" and "Baby, let me do that for you." And finally, "Now be careful honey...I don't want you getting hurt."

One time of being called sweetie, baby, and honey, was enough for Mrs. Brown. She politely invited me to sit at the table with her and told me she was an adult, not a child, and she expected to be treated with dignity. To be certain that I understood, she told me if I called her baby, or sweetie, or honey, one more time I would be asked to leave her home.

Lesson 3: Your appearance is the first message you give to the clients.

I adore wearing makeup, dangling earrings, and bright fingernail polish. And I love having fiery red hair one week and precious pink the next, and so on. The more hair colors I use, the more I like it. It speaks for how I feel and who I am.

When I had my job interview, my hair was its

natural color, brown. I passed the interview and personality test with flying colors. They also had me read the employee handbook, and it didn't mention anything about hair color.

I did great my first week on the job. The second week, I went on duty with streaks of precious pink in my new fiery red hair color.

When my client saw me, she told me to get out of her house. She called the office and told them she was sure I was on drugs because of my red hair with pink stripes.

Different generations, different thoughts.

Lesson 4: Clear Communication

I knocked on the door. No one answered. I knocked again, loud this time. No answer. I opened the door and went inside. I spent my next five minutes convincing my client, who was hard of hearing and at times forgetful, not to call the police. I told her I wasn't breaking and entering, but that I worked for her.

I pointed to my name badge, then the clock, and she giggled.

She asked me to write on a big piece of paper, in big

letters, the days and times that I would be in her home and tape it on her refrigerator.

I did what she requested; then I politely asked if she would wear her hearing aid on the days I worked. She giggled and agreed.

Observing, Recording, and Reporting

Judge: "The prosecution may call its first witness."

Prosecuting Attorney: "I would like

to call Judy Lynn Norris to the stand."

[Bailiff takes the witness to the witness stand.]

Clerk: "Please stand. Raise your right hand. Do you promise that the testimony you shall give in the case before this court shall be the truth, the whole truth, and nothing but the truth, so help you, God?"

"I do."

Clerk: "Please state your first and last name."

"Judy Norris."

Clerk: "You may be seated."

Reporter: "Please spell your last name for the record."

"N-o-r-r-i-s"

The Prosecuting Attorney stands and directs his questions at the witness. "What is your occupation? And where do you work?"

"I'm a Certified Home Health Aide, and I work for Mattie's Private Duty Agency in Conway, Arkansas."

"Did you work for Mattie's Private Duty Agency and take care of Mrs. Joan Wallace, from February 4, 2017, to December 7, 2018?"

"Yes, sir."

"Is it correct that you clocked in and out of work on her private telephone according to the rules of your agency?"

"Yes, sir."

The attorney shows Miss Norris some papers. "Are these your timesheets? And, if so, are they signed by you and Mrs. Wallace?"

"Yes, sir. Except for the last two weeks that I took care of Mrs. Wallace; she couldn't hold a pen, sign her name, or even make a mark because of hand tremors."

Next, he gives a document to the witness. "Would you please read out loud what you wrote about Mrs. Wallace on December 7, the day before she died?"

"Mrs. Wallace was not able to hold her fork or spoon to feed herself because of weakness and severe tremors in both hands. I spoon-fed her. She ate only three bites of scrambled egg and a few bites of toast for breakfast. She refused to eat anything the rest of the day. She slept most of the day. When she talked her voice was weak, and she had a blank expression on her face. She called me Gladys, her deceased daughter's name. Mrs. Wallace's niece and a man came to visit her. I left the room during their visit at the niece's request. I reported my observations to Sue Smith, R.N. Supervisor."

"Your Honor, I ask that these records be admitted as evidence for the prosecution."

Judge: "Does the defense have any objections or questions?"

Defending Attorney: "No, Your Honor."

Judge: "Request granted. The witness is excused."

Mrs. Wallace had willed her entire estate to the state-owned Human Development Center that had taken care of her profoundly disabled son for 20 years. The day before Mrs. Wallace died, a niece from out of state came to visit her. The niece's attorney went with her to Mrs. Wallace's home. They testified in court that Mrs. Wallace signed a new Will that named the niece as the beneficiary to Mrs. Wallace's entire estate.

Because of the home care aide's observations, documentation, and reporting, the judge ruled that the Will naming the niece as beneficiary was invalid.

Before they left the courtroom, the judge filed charges against the niece and her attorney.

Different Cultures

I remember going to Spanish class each day and getting excited to learn a new language. It was fun and interesting, and when the agency told me I would be getting a Spanish speaking client, I was thrilled. Her name was Mrs. Mariana Martinez, and she lived with her sister-in-law, Lucia Martinez, who could speak very limited English.

Mariana was aphasic (without speech) because of a stroke and couldn't swallow food. Lucia fed her through a feeding tube. Mariana's hospital bed was in the living room so she could look out the front window. She could transfer to a wheelchair with help, and she enjoyed sitting outside on the front porch of their small home.

They were sweet and kind, and I enjoyed the job.

However, I soon learned that my job could be much smoother if I learned how to do it without speaking Spanish. I couldn't tell if they were amused with me or irritated.

So, from then on, I continued my job using a lot of nonverbal communication. Hand gestures, eye contact, and an occasional Spanish word took me a long way. I was able to befriend Mariana and her sister, Lucia. I had the care routine down, and everything thing went smooth, until one day, something changed.

I walked into the house on a Wednesday morning, ready to work, when Mariana glared at me.

It was like a switch had flipped. Mariana wasn't the same person I knew. She fumbled for her water glass on the bedside table and knocked it to the floor. As I bent over to wipe up the water, she threw her pillow at me. I looked up at her face, and tears were streaming down her face. I knew that a drastic change in behavior could mean a serious health issue.

"Que pasa? Dolar?" I asked quietly.

She nodded yes and pointed to her head.

I called her nephew. He quickly came and asked me to go with them to Urgent Care. I called the office and got permission to go.

By the time we arrived at Urgent Care, Mariana wasn't responding to anyone's voice, but she flinched when the doctor tested her for pain. The doctor immediately called an ambulance. Mariana was transported to the Emergency Room, where she was diagnosed with a brain tumor.

I'm glad I could speak a little Spanish, but I learned it wasn't the language I spoke or the color of my skin, it was my skills and the care I gave Mariana that made the greatest difference.

COPD

"Bring me a cigarette," he said between short puffs of oxygen. His face gleamed a shiny pale from his chin to his cheeks, and a dark gray circled his deep-set brown eyes. His chest rattled with secretions, and every breath was a struggle.

I shook my head and pointed to the "No Smoking" sign I had drawn and posted on the bedroom door.

He knew he'd be struggling a lot harder without his

oxygen to breathe. He once told me oxygen was an addiction just like his cigarettes were, but the oxygen saved his life, and the cigarettes destroyed it.

He raised his clubbed fingers with blue-tinged fingernails and snapped his thumb and middle finger without a sound. "If I can't have a cigarette, then bring me a bottle of whiskey." He laughed a deep-throated laugh as his shoulders and barrel chest barely moved up and down.

I grinned to acknowledge his humor. "The Hospice nurse said you could have a beer if you wanted one. And my supervisor told me I could bring you a beer, but she suggested you open it."

"Sounds like the directions on my Care Plan for my medicines."

I nodded and brought him some chips, a can of beer, and a glass.

He ignored the glass and pushed opened the tab and took a sip out of the can. "Good stuff," he said. He took another sip, then rested a minute. "My wife would be sitting beside me if I'd had enough sense years ago to stop smoking." He stopped to pull some air into his lungs. "But I didn't know about second-hand smoke."

There was a long pause. "The good thing is, I'll soon be joining my wife and my father and my mother in the forever that I call Heaven." He sucked in some air and blew it out through pursed lips. "I had a nice dream about my wife last night."

"I'm glad," I replied.

"I appreciate you. You're an excellent aide," he said. "Would you do me a favor?"

"It depends on the favor."

"I want you to bring your oldest son here to meet me."

His request took me off guard, but I liked the idea. "I have to get permission from my supervisor."

"I already got it because I want to talk to that young man about smoking cigarettes." He glanced up at me with tears in his eyes. "Maybe I'm the one who can knock some sense into him so that he won't end up like me."

Parkinson's Disease

Clear
+
Vivid

66 **T**he more I expect, the more unhappy I am going to be. The more I accept, the more serene I am." *Michael J. Fox*

Michael J. Fox is one of my heroes. He, and Alan Alda, and the estimated seven to ten million people in the world who are living with Parkinson's Disease.

My name is Susan Matthews. I'm 68 years old. And

I have Parkinson's disease.

I was diagnosed four years ago with the textbook symptoms: Change in my posture, walk, and facial expressions. I also had tremors on one side of my body, but the prescribed medication controlled the tremors, and I continued to work as an administrative assistant in our local Junior College.

Gradually, my symptoms worsened, and I had to quit work. Soon after I quit, I met another hero; a wonderful, spunky home care aide, Camila Gonzales.

Camila helped with some of the simple activities of daily living that I could no longer do by myself; bathing, grocery shopping, and changing my bed linen. She listened patiently, without interrupting, to my whining and complaining. Her words were always kind and positive.

Camila also encouraged me to get out of my house and socialize with people. She said she'd take me in her car. Each time I considered it, images of people staring at me and seeing the pitiful look in their eyes flashed in my mind. I refused to go anywhere but to the doctor's office—until November 18, 2018. That's the day Camila introduced me to Alan Alda and Michael J. Fox.

The introduction was through the internet's Clear + Vivid with Alan Alda and Michael J. Fox: *How to Keep Going When Life Gives You Speed Bumps.*

I was immediately captivated by the content of the podcast and the voices.

The richness of Alan Alda's voice, luxurious and warm, instantly comforted me and dissolved my stress from a miserable night of fighting forces from the dark side. And Michael J. Fox's low, soft but powerful voice vibrated through the speakers with an emotional strength that sent chills through my body.

They spoke openly as their personal experiences seeped into their conversation.

I felt like I was sitting at the same table with them.

I listened intently for almost forty-five minutes. As usual, my hands shook uncontrollably, but my mind stayed alert and steady.

When the podcast was over, I wiped the tears from my eyes and told Camila that I wanted to go to the Senior Citizen's Center to have lunch and find out about their activities.

As I write this sentence, there is no definite cure for Parkinson's disease. However, there is hope, thanks to the millions of dollars that have gone to research from the Michael J. Fox Foundation. And I found peace and acceptance from Alan Alda's "Clear + Vivid" podcast.

About the Authors

Elise Mathis attends the University of Central Arkansas in Conway, Arkansas, where she is studying political science. She enjoys acting, singing, and writing. Elise is the co-author's granddaughter.

Mimi Mathis is a registered nurse with years of experience in Home Health. She lives in Fayetteville, Arkansas. She enjoys animals, music, and writing. Her greatest joy in life has been raising her three sons with her husband, Jack, and having seven grandchildren.

About the Illustrator

Lilly Mathis attends Kent State University in Kent, Ohio, where she is studying fashion design. She enjoys sewing, designing clothes, art, and soccer. Lilly is another one of Mimi's granddaughters.

About the Book Cover

Darene Bingham Loyd drew the book cover. Darene is a registered nurse with a Bachelor of Science in Health Education. She taught Certified Nursing Students for thirty-one years in a Vocational Technical Center. Darene is Mimi's sister.

http://www.aboutgivingcare.com/

Made in the USA
Monee, IL
02 September 2019